GOOM

JOSHUA WRIGHT

ALLEN&UNWIN

Come one, come all!
Visit www.joshuawright.net

First published in 2004

Allen & Unwin
83 Alexander Street
Crows Nest NSW 2065
Australia
Phone: (61 2) 8425 0100
Fax: (61 2) 9906 2218
Email: info@allenandunwin.com
Web: www.allenandunwin.com

National Library of Australia
Cataloguing-in-Publication entry:

Wright, Joshua, 1973– .
  Goom.

  For children aged 10–14 years.
  ISBN 1 74114 435 3.

  I. Title

A823.4

Cover and text design by Tou-Can Design
Set in 14 pt Stone Sans by Tou-Can Design
Printed in Australia by McPherson's Printing Group, Maryborough, Victoria

10 9 8 7 6 5 4 3 2 1

ANATOMY

Goom

Who was Goom? Well, he was just like you and me really. Except maybe a little shorter, a little greener, and a little more homicidal.

He lived in the county of Yeedlebeetle-beetle. You say it just as it is spelt: 'Yeedle-beetle-beetle', except faster.

Yeedlebeetlebeetle County was a cold, windswept moor. Yes, miles and miles of moor. Wherever you looked, there was just more and more moor. Yeedlebeetle-beetlians made their homes on this soggy, overgrown wilderness.

The folks of Yeedlebeetlebeetle were the standard mix of yokels, bumpkins and rubes you'd expect to find in a place no thinking person would live. Especially since the whole county was owned by an insanely evil wizard.

Pernikous the Necromancer was his name.

His profession, death magic, had worked out well for him. Necromancy was all about chopping up dead critters and putting them in spells, potions, minces and so on.

Pernikous could use anything from mashed bugs and splattered birds right up to dead monsters to magic up whatever took his fancy. He loved creating zombies and talking skulls and other such horrors.

AHHHH.
HOME, SWEET
BLOODY
HOME.

CASA
DE
LUNATIC

He even once had a passionate love affair with a woman he built out of dead chickens and an old sewing machine. Her name was Geraldine.

Pernikous made his money with taxes collected from Yeedlebeetlebeetlians for allowing them to live on his land.

HARRY THE GOLEM

I'M JUST GOOD AT MAKING FRIENDS... LITERALLY.

MRS. USEFUL

BUTT BRAIN

No one dared defy him. If they did, they'd soon find a gang of ghouls on their doorstep. Indeed, old Pernikous had everything worked out to suit him.

But one fateful day Pernikous decided a militia of moaning minions was not enough. He wanted a creature more intelligent. Something he could order about and beat when he got angry. Something no self-respecting wizard should be without.

A familiar.

Familiars are very popular among magic-using folk. Witches like cats. Wizards sometimes have toads. Warlocks prefer imps or gargoyles. Necromancers, though, are special. They can make their own.

IF YOUR JOB HAD A FAMILIAR, THIS IS WHAT IT WOULD BE...

YAP YAP YIP YAP YAP YIP YAP

BOOKWORM

WEASEL

LITTLE YIPPY DOG

LAWYER

TEACHER

LIBRARIAN

COW

SLIPPERY EEL

TURKEY

FARMER

CRIMINAL

PROFESSIONAL FOOTBALLER

HAMMERHEAD SHARK

OLD BOOT

BUMBLE BEE

CARPENTER

POLICEMAN

COMPUTER SYSTEMS ANALYST

That night Pernikous set to work.
And after much chopping, hacking,
rending and blending, he was done.

'I name you…Goom!' said Pernikous proudly. 'My wish shall be your command. You understand?'

Goom seemed confused.

'Understand?' Pernikous said again. 'You'll do exactly as I say.'

'Ahh,' Goom nodded. 'You'll do exactly as I say.'

'No – exactly as *I* say!' Pernikous pointed to himself.

Goom pointed to himself too. 'Yes, I understand – exactly as *I* say.'

'No, you dunce! Isn't your brain plugged in properly? When I say *me*, I mean…' Pernikous stopped. There was something wrong with his new creation's face. The corner of his mouth was twisted. It turned upwards, almost like a smile.

But it was even more than that –
Goom was smirking. A sly, toothy,
sarcastic smirk.

'Hey, you know *exactly* what I mean!'
Goom giggled.

'Enough! I warn you, any disobedience
and I'll boil you up. Now get into the
kitchen and cook my supper.'

'Yes... *Master.*' Goom shuffled off.' You
lousy, pot-licking, chalk-chewing...'

'What?!'

'Nothing!' The little fellow flashed a
smile.

When it was finally cooked, Pernikous's
supper tasted awful. No one washed up
either. That night, and many nights after
that, Pernikous came to think that
making Goom had not been
such a good idea.

WHAT'S
A 'FREUDIAN?'

He was right too.

LIFE WITH PERNIKOUS

Over the following months Pernikous began to regret creating Goom at all. A familiar was meant to take orders willingly and fulfil its master's every command. Instead Goom was a disobedient skulker and often needed swatting before he'd do anything.

For example, it was Goom's job every night to lurk about the county. After all the Yeedlebeetlebeetlians were in bed, Pernikous made him go out looking for dead things. Goom crept about grabbing fetid foxes, battered birds and rotten rabbits. He had a spatula to scrape up squashed things and a spade to dig up buried things.

On this particular night his bag felt light. All he'd managed to find was an arm and three goldfish. When he finally got back to the tower, Pernikous wasn't impressed.

'*This* is all you've got?' he said as he rummaged through the bag. 'How am I supposed to make blood-curdling zombies with *goldfish*?'

Goom shrugged. 'Maybe you could use them as their eyeballs?'

'You useless wretch! You've let me down again! Get off and cook my supper, I'm starving!'

Goom cooked Pernikous's usual: a roast ham, a cherry pie, candy corn and squid. He made sure to spit on all the food and drop it on the dirty floor several times. Pernikous could never taste the difference. Goom rang the dinner bell when it was ready.

Pernikous sat down to eat, hoeing into the ham like a pig.

'Hang on,' he said licking his plate. 'Where's my cherry pie?'

'I don't know,' said Goom.

SEE? THIS IS WHAT HAPPENS WHEN YOU OVERFEED US.

Pernikous's eyes narrowed. 'What's that red stuff around your mouth?'

'Umm...lipstick?'

'I didn't know you wore lipstick.'

Goom shrugged. 'I didn't either until now.'

Pernikous looked across the table. 'Where's my candy corn?'

'I don't know.'

THERE'D BETTER BE A BRILLIANT EXPLANATION FOR ALL THIS, GOOM!

'Why are your hands covered in candy?'

'Um...that's just my moisturiser.'

Pernikous raised a sceptical brow. 'In that case, explain the tentacle hanging out your mouth! You've eaten my squid too!'

Goom gobbled it down quickly. 'No, that was just my tongue. Sometimes I pant, you know, like a dog. It keeps me cool.'

Pernikous threw back his chair. 'Just how stupid do you think I am?'

'...I'd say about a seven.'

YOU KNOW, IT WAS THE DARNEDEST THING, I SLIPPED OVER IN THE KITCHEN AND THE FOOD JUST FELL IN MY MOUTH.

Pernikous stormed out of the room. He went into the kitchen and got some pig snout leftovers from the fridge. 'That little creep,' he grumbled. 'Eat my dinner right out from under me, will he?'

Goom came tip-tapping in after him.

'Good snouts?' he asked.

'Yes,' Pernikous grunted. 'No thanks to you.'

'Oh, I wouldn't say that. They're my *special* recipe snouts.'

Soaking into the bread was oozy yellow snot.

'Boogies! Bleach!' Pernikous threw the food at him. 'You little swine! Go chuck them down the well!' He belted him across the head. 'And get out to the wheelhouse too! I've got a lot to do tonight.'

'...Yes, master,' Goom rubbed his sore scone. 'You fat, wart-ridden, camel-faced, toilet-sniffing–'

'What?!'

'Nothing!' he chimed.

THE WHEELHOUSE

IT'S CALLED THAT COS THERE'S A WHEEL INSIDE.

KEEP OUT!

Next to the tower stood a shed. Inside the shed was a huge wooden wheel connected to cogs and pulleys that ran up into the tower. When the wheel turned it acted as a generator that powered Pernikous's bone cookers and zombie machines.

Chained to the wheel was a big old bear called Rosy. She had been a slave in the wheelhouse all her life, but it had never seemed to bother her.

'Time to start up, Rosy,' Goom said as he patted Rosy's coat.

'Okay, Goomy.' Rosy nodded and, with a lurch, began turning.

Goom left the bear to her work and went out back with the snouts.

The well stank like the compost heap from hell. For years Pernikous had been throwing his junk down it, things like guts, slime, bones, leftover bodies, failed experiments, magical waste, rotten food and old clothes. Goom shuddered to think of the horrible magic stew going on down there.

He tossed the meat into the well and hurried away. He was sure he heard it burp.

TRY LIVING WITH ONE OF THEM IN YOUR BACKYARD.

DANGER: TOXIC GARBAGE

Push Comes, Goom Shoves

Pernikous was busy in his workshop. A sudden inspiration had hit him. He was building something. Something big.

'What are you up to, Master?' asked Goom. 'Another zombie?'

'No.' Pernikous hammered away the mess of nuts, guts and bolts.

'Is it a ghoul? Or a golem perhaps?'

'No.'

'Are you making yourself another girlfriend? I think you've been alone too long–'

'No!' he snapped.

'... A boyfriend then?'

'Watch it!' Pernikous clonked him with a spanner. 'If you must know I'm building *your* replacement.'

'Replace *me*? What for?'

'Because you're a useless, lazy, snide little sneak. I need a *new* familiar.' He pointed to a pair of huge arms hanging on the workshop wall. 'And its first order of business will be to wring your neck! When I'm finished making this brute, he'll be able to beat up on villagers and do all the heavy work. I can even get rid of that bear too.'

'You mean Rosy?' Goom shuddered.

'Where else will I get a ticker big enough to fit it? I'm taking the bear's. In fact, run out right now and unlock your fuzzy friend.' Pernikous tossed Goom his precious keys.

WHAT DID I TELL YA? I'M EVERYTHING THIS NEW GUY'S GUNNA BE AND MORE.

'Bring her in here. I think it's time she
and I had a *heart* to *heart* talk.'

'I won't!' Goom stamped his foot.
'Rosy is my friend!'

Pernikous wrapped a fist around
Goom's throat. 'You will or I'll strangle
you myself!'

Goom snapped his teeth down on his
master's oily paw. Pernikous yelped and
dropped him. Goom zipped out of the
room with the keys. The necromancer
was furious.

'Come back here, you traitor!'

Goom wasn't listening. He rushed outside to the wheelhouse. Rosy was there, still dutifully walking in circles. Goom jumped up and unlocked her shackles.

'What are you doing, Goomy?'

'You've got to get out of here, Rosy!' The chains slid off the bear's back. 'Pernikous is going to cut you up!'

'Me?' Rosy blinked. 'No. The Master loves me. I turn the wheel.'

Goom pulled desperately on her coat. 'He *is*, Rosy. You've got to believe me!' He led the confused bear outside into the dark.

AWW, HAPPIER TIMES.

Pernikous burst outside with his bone saw.

'Come here, Goom! It's no use hiding!'

Goom and Rosy watched from the bushes down by the well. Pernikous thumped about, scouring the yard.

'He's going to spot us soon,' Goom whispered. 'He's really honked up this time.'

Rosy scowled. 'You shouldn't provoke the Master, Goomy. Running a whole county is a lot of pressure.'

'Pressure? He doesn't do *a thing* for Yeedlebeetlebeetle. He's based an entire career on making a menace of himself!'

PSSST! GOOMY.
I THINK I LEFT
THE WHEELHOUSE
LIGHT ON.
I REALLY SHOULD
GO BACK UP
THERE...

ROSY, PLEASE.
LET'S PRIORITISE,
SHALL WE?

Rosy shook her head. 'The Master's not bad. He just loves his work.'

Suddenly Pernikous loomed over them. 'Aha, here you are!' he shouted triumphantly, grabbing Goom by the tail.

Goom cried to Rosy. 'See? Look how bad the master is! He's going to saw me up!'

The bear stood up from behind the bushes. 'Master, please, what's the matter?'

'The matter?' Pernikous growled. 'That's between me and my familiar, isn't it, Goom?'

Rosy stepped closer, paws outstretched. 'Master? Goom? Please, let's all try to calm down here...'

Now remember, Rosy was a huge bear, so when she came towards Pernikous, the old devil quivered.

ONE FALSE MOVE BEAR, AND THE...THE... WELL, WHATEVER THE HELL HE IS GETS IT.

SUPA SHARP BONE HACKER

COME ON ROSY, CLAW HIM TO PIECES!

'Wait! Don't get any funny ideas...'
Pernikous staggered backwards, drop-
ping Goom and his saw. The menacing
maw of the well gaped behind him.

Goom grabbed the bone saw. He swung fiercely at his master's leg, chopping off his foot. Pernikous howled in pain and toppled backward over the well's edge.

'Goom! What are you doing? Help me!'

'No!'

'What?' Pernikous clung to the edge. 'I order you to help me!'

'No – I will ***not***, you wart-ridden, weasel-faced, garlic-breathed, badly-dressed, greasy-haired, bow-legged, pot-bellied, pigeon-toed PINHEAD!'

Goom stamped on Pernikous's fingers and the necromancer fell tumbling, down, down, down into the murky green and disappeared.

The well burped. Goom was positive this time.

CHANGES, SOME GOOD, SOME VERY BAD

BRAND SPANKING, NEW LOOK TOWER AFTER A RIGHT-ROYAL MAKEOVER, SPRING-CLEANING AND BACKYARD BLITZ.

Things around the tower changed after that. Pernikous was gone. Goom was happy. Rosy tried to be happy too.

'But he kept you as a slave,' Goom tried to explain. 'He deserved it, Rosy. We've done the whole of Yeedlebeetlebeetle a favour. He was rotten to his rotted core.'

'The poor Master,' the bear sighed. 'It just seems wrong.'

'No, Rosy. We've just begun setting things *right*.'

REMEMBER THOUGH GOOMY, IT'S WHAT'S <u>INSIDE</u> THAT COUNTS.

WELL, SINCE THAT'D BE <u>US</u>, I COULDN'T AGREE MORE.

Together they made renovations. First the wheelhouse was demolished. Then they made a bonfire out of Pernikous's cruel cookers and machines. Rosy re-buried the corpses the necromancer had kept for parts. Plus they made new cushions for the sofa and converted the automatic blood drainer into a juice maker.

The two kicked back in their newly refurbished lounge room. Rosy looked up from her freshly squeezed OJ.

'Mmm, the master liked a nice drink too. I think he would be proud of what we've done.'

'Are you nutty?' Goom gagged on his grape juice. 'He'd pop his gourd if he saw all this!'

'No, you're too hard on him. I wish he were here right now.'

Goom was shocked. 'You *miss* Pernikous?'

'I even wrote a song about him.' Rosy stood up. 'It's called *Pernikous, my Pudding...*'

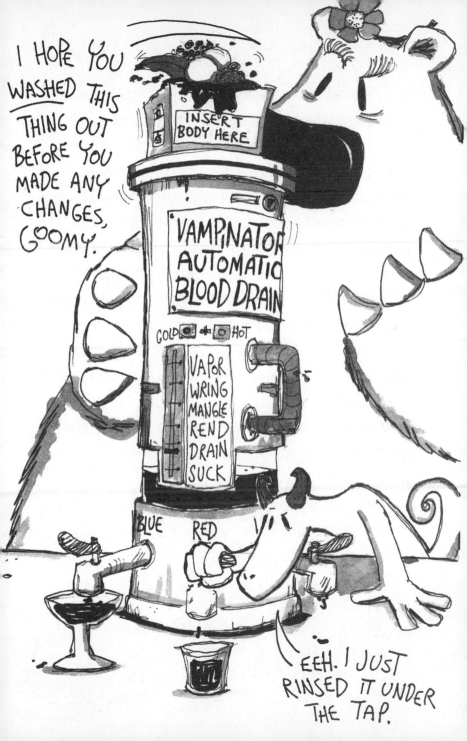

'Pernikous, sweet pudding! I miss you so much and I am so sorry what Goomy did was not very good and it makes me sad to think you got your foot chopped off and fell down that well where you are not feeling well because you are dead and probably fell on your head, I saw you with the saw and I know you were mad and that makes me sad because I am glad that you chose me for your wheel and to help you work and it is such a perk that even though you chain me up it is nice to be useful, I need you to know that I miss you so and when they say you are foul it makes

GADZOOKS!
HOW CAN ONE SO
KIND INFLICT SUCH
CRUELTY?!

*me howl because I know if you weren't
such a swine you would be kind! Pernikous,
sweet pudding! Pernikous, sweet–'*

Goom clamped his hand over Rosy's
mouth. 'You're freaking me out!'

Rosy sat back down. 'I just miss him,
that's all.'

Goom decided not to argue and let
Rosy get over it herself. Personally he
was happy Pernikous was gone for good.

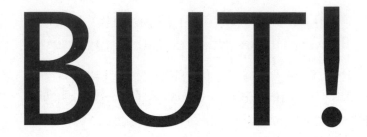

Goom had forgotten one very important thing: if you *are* going to get someone, you have to make sure they *stay* got.

Or else later that night during a terrible thunderstorm...

Rosy and Goom sat by the fire playing Operation™ when there came a strange rapping at the door. Goom got up, wondering who it could be on such a night.

'Pernikous?!' he gasped. *'IT'S YOU!'*

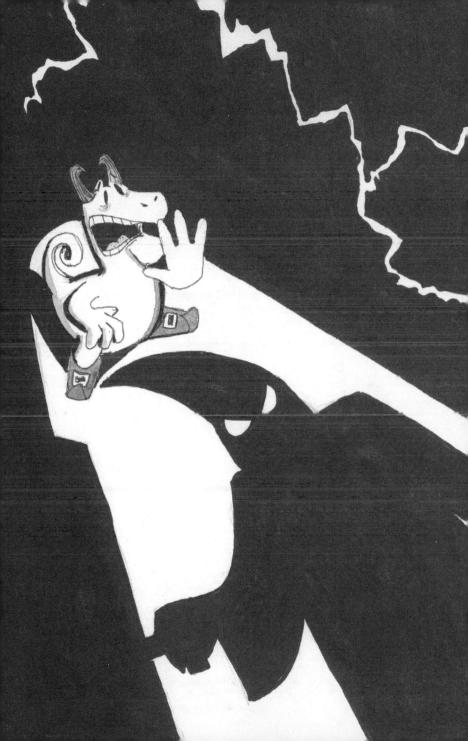

It was the necromancer all right, but not the same one they knew. On the doorstep stood a skeleton dressed in a filthy, worm-eaten robe. The eyes in his skull burned like hot coals. Slime, sinew and mud covered his whole body. His brain oozed out of his cracked, bony head where wisps of hair still grew. His skin was gone, exposing his guts and stringy muscles. Some organs had been eaten by maggots (which could still be spotted on him). Even the foot that had been chopped off had reattached itself.

'I've had a little accident,' he said quietly. 'But all I can remember is going out to the well.'

'M-m-Master?' Goom was dumbfounded. 'C-can I get you anything?'

'Yes, please,' he said politely. 'A cup of tea, thanks.'

The necromancer was back. Whatever had happened to him in that well they could only dare imagine.

MISSING BODY, EMPTY HEAD

Pernikous tried to think.

'...Well, I know I'm a wizard...and I own this whole moor. I remember you Goom and you, umm...bear. I know we live here and make magic stuff...I remember that you're my servants.'

'Go on,' Goom said nervously. 'Tell us what you remember about the last few days.'

'I...I think was making something... something big. I sent Goom outside for some reason, but when he didn't come back I got worried. I went out looking for him and...' he stopped. 'Ummm...' He scratched his brain with a bony finger. '...The rest is a blur.'

Goom sighed with relief. He poured some tea. Pernikous drank it, but it just dribbled out the bottom of his jaw.

'So why are you like *this*?' Rosy sobbed. 'You poor Master, why are you so...so...gooey?'

Pernikous was confused. 'What do you mean *gooey*?'

He went to the mirror.

'AAAARRR RGGGGH HHHH!!!'

'What's wrong with me? I look like I've been backstroking in an acid bath!' He grabbed Goom. 'Tell me how this happened!'

'I don't know, Master!' Goom choked. Clearly the old, evil Pernikous wasn't far below his maggoty exterior. 'We didn't see anything!'

Pernikous dropped Goom and began to pace. It seemed the necromancer had

HONESTLY MASTER, I HAVE NO IDEA HOW YOU BECAME SUCH A TWISTED FREAK!

PSSST, WHATEVER YOU DO GOOMY, DON'T MENTION THE BROWN OOZE DRIBBLING DOWN HIS LEG. I'M PRETTY SURE IT'S JUST _MUD_, BUT—

—YEH, I HEAR YA. I DON'T WANT TO KNOW EITHER.

fallen victim to his own gory magic. The wheels of his mind turned furiously, trying to figure a way out of his slimy state.

'. . . I think you look nice, Master,' Rosy tried to comfort him. 'Your guts are very well laid out.'

Goom agreed. 'Yes, very colourful. You could call it zombie chic. Plus I never realised you had such refined features. Your cheekbones are so. . . umm. . . I think a centipede just crawled inside your brain.'

'I can't live like this!' Pernikous threaded the bug back out of his head and squished it on the floor. 'No women will want to go out with me!'

'We can *make* you a girl' Goom said, trying not to laugh. 'We'll find another just like Geraldine the sewing machine. Why, she'll be the prettiest reanimated corpse in the county. Yes, Beauty and the Beast.'

POTENTIAL HOMEMADE

DEAD CAT KATE

MELON HEAD MARYLIN

BONY BETTY

'Me? A beast? So you *do* think I'm ugly! Oh, it's no use!' Pernikous flew out of the room bawling, 'I'm ugly! I'm ugly! I'm ugly!' and leaving a bloody trail behind him.

Goom sighed. 'Well, this is all very... interesting.' He went over to the fireplace and grabbed the coal shovel. 'Now I'm going to have to do this all over again.'

GIRLFRIENDS FOR PERNIKOUS.

← JODY 'PEELED OFF THE ROADY'

KISSY CORPSE ←

THIS ONES' MY FAVOURITE. C'MON, GIVE ME SOME SUGAR, SWEETLIPS! ↓

SMOOCH∴

'Do what?' asked Rosy.

'I've got to finish him off before his memory comes back. When it does, well, we're both dead meat.' He took a few practice swings with the shovel. 'One quick knock on his noggin should do the trick.'

'No!' Rosy was horrified. 'The poor Master! We have to help him! He's upstairs crying his eyes out and you just want to be meaner to him? No, this our chance to all be happy again!'

'Happy?!'

'Yes, just like it was. Me in the wheelhouse and you in the workshop.'

Goom groaned. 'I'll be happy again – right after I put this shovel across the Master's head.'

♫ HERE PERNY, PERNY, PERNY... ♫

So off he went. The stairs
creaked as Goom crept up them.
The plan was to get Pernikous from
behind. Rosy followed nervously after,
still feeling very bad about the whole
thing. They could hear the Master
rustling about in his study.

'Try not to hurt him too much,' Rosy
whispered.

Goom rolled his eyes. He readied the
shovel and peeked inside the door.

UH OH. HE'S GOT THAT CRAZY LOOK IN HIS EYES!

'Aha, Goom!
There you are!'
Pernikous boomed.
'I should have known!
I should have guessed all along!'

Goom felt a lump in his throat.
'...G-g-g-guess what, Master?' He hid
the shovel behind his back.

'The answer, of course. See?' Ooze
trickled onto the *Extra Fancy Necromancy*
book he held out before him. 'This is it,
right here! It says we have to find a rare
and mysterious magic that will bring me
back to normal.'

Rosy clapped her paws. 'That's
wonderful!'

Goom was a little less thrilled. 'But
how, Master? Do you even know where
this "rare and mysterious magic" is?'

'It is in this very county,' Pernikous
showed him, 'kept in a windswept chapel
only a few days journey away. Here, see?
I've even mapped out our route...'

Across the moor, over the river, through the
town, past the keep and to the cliffs, where
stands the Abbey of the Broken Heart.

Pernikous's rotted teeth stretched to a
smile. 'Start packing.'

By morning they were ready. Pernikous always travelled in a big flashy caravan pulled by Rosy. Painted on the side was:

PERNIKOUS THE NECROMANCER!
DARK MASTER OF DEATH MAGIC!
LOOKING FOR AN EXCITING CAREER? CURIOUS ABOUT SCIENCE? JOIN THE NECROMANTIC SCHOOL OF ANATOMY! BECOME A CADAVER AND MAKE BIG MONEY! ENQUIRE WITHIN.

'Let's roll!' Pernikous hollered.

He cracked on the reins and Rosy hauled the caravan off up the road across the moor. Their quest had begun: onward to the Abbey of the Broken Heart.

Goom sat next to Pernikous. 'Master, your slimy bum is leaving puddles on the seat!'

'Feel free to get off and walk,' said Pernikous.

74

The caravan trundled on for the rest of the day. The few people who saw it knew enough to stay clear.

That evening the travellers looked
for somewhere quiet to set up camp.
Pernikous knew of a good spot, but
when they got there another caravan
had taken it. A donkey wagon was
parked on the crest of the hill. Beside it
sat a woman by a campfire. She called
to them in a croaky voice. 'Stop, friends!
Come join another weary traveller in a
cup of hot mush!'

'Who is this old crow?' Pernikous
grouched. 'Doesn't she know who I am?'

'Perhaps she's a fan?' said Goom.

'Come on. Let's stop and say hello,'
Rosy said, and pulled over.

IF YOU THINK I'M UGLY NOW, YOU SHOULD SEE ME WITHOUT MAKE-UP!

When they joined the woman by the fire, Goom got a better look. She was the nastiest, freakiest, creepiest slab of female he'd even seen – and he worked with the rotting dead.

'Welcome Pernikous,' she said. 'You're right on time.'

'Do I know you?'

'Don't you recognise me? I'm Eva Braunstein, the wicked witch from two counties over. We met at last year's Evil Christmas party. I've been waiting for you. I know all about your accident.'

Goom gulped. 'ALL about?'

'I saw it all commercial-free on my crystal ball.' Eva's ugly mug gave a gap-toothed grin. 'I've made a deal with a curious stranger. They told me you'd be coming this way.'

'What kind of deal?' said Rosy.

'What kind of stranger?' said Goom.

'I wasn't talking to you two,' Eva scowled. 'Pernikous, come into my caravan. I shall reveal *all*.'

Goom spat. 'Master, yuck! She wants to take her clothes off!'

Pernikous shook his head. 'Sorry, lady. You're not my type.'

'No, you dolt! I mean I will answer all your questions.'

'Well, why didn't you say so?' Pernikous got up. 'Let's go.'

Eva smiled a secret, evil smile. She led him inside her caravan. Rosy watched her lock the door behind them.

'I don't like her, Goomy. She's up to something.'

Like a spring Goom leapt up from the campfire.

'She's going to squeal on us! Come on, this is our chance!'

Goom ran around and unhitched the witch's donkey.

Now Rosy realised what he meant. 'Oh, no. You're not trying to kill the Master *again*? You're crazy!'

'It's going to work this time, I can feel it!' said Goom. He ripped out the caravan's brake handle.

'But, Goomy, the Master has changed. He's much less mean now. We can all be happy if we work at it together!'

'No! It's *my* way or the highway – with no brakes!'

Goom pushed the caravan's wheel. It only needed a nudge to start it rolling down the hill. Rosy watched it rumble past her. Quickly picking up speed, it tore along, bouncing over rock and gravel.

OH, GOOMY! LOOK
WHAT YOU'VE DONE!

I KNOW! AREN'T
YOU PROUD
OF ME?

CAUTION:
STEEP
DESCENT

It lurched to one side and
began to flip and tumble over.
Bits flew everywhere. The wheels
snapped off their axle. Finally, with a
great crash, it slammed against a tree
and splintered into a thousand pieces.

Goom and Rosy hurried down to
inspect the wreck. On the way he
spotted one of Pernikous's slimy legs.

'Must have broken off,' he chuckled.
'I guess he won't be needing that again.'

'That's what you think!'

It was Pernikous! He stood up on his one good leg. 'That woman should be ashamed of herself! Her caravan is a death trap! Look, now I've lost a limb!'

But Eva lay face down in the mud. The witch was as dead as a doornail.

'But did she tell you anything?' Goom asked nervously.

'She didn't get a chance,' said Pernikous. 'Frankly I'm glad she's gone. That chick was nuts.'

Goom faked his relief. 'Well, we thought you were a goner too, didn't we, Rosy?'

'You poor, poor Master,' said the bear, shooting a scowl at Goom.

'What are you doing with the brake handle?' said Pernikous.

'Oh, this?' Goom said quickly. 'I was trying to save you, of course. I yanked so hard trying to pull up the caravan, the brake snapped off completely. Luckily I managed to slow it down though.'

'Lucky?' Pernikous brushed himself off. 'No, Goom. The truth is in my current state I'm actually quite bouncy. It must have something to do with all these springy organs.' He poked a finger into his insides and sure enough, they bounced back.

BOI-OI-ING!

...Over the River...

Pernikous couldn't get his leg to go back on. He tried glue, nails and string, but it was just too slimy to stick. Finally Goom just hammered a block of wood onto his stump so the necromancer could still limp around.

I SWEAR GOOM, ONE MORE "SHIVER ME TIMBERS" OUT OF YOU AND I'LL BREAK THIS WOODEN LEG ACROSS YOUR HEAD!

AYE AYE, CAP'N.

PERNIKOUS

'There you go, Peg-leg. Good as new!'
Pernikous was not impressed.

The next day's travel began peacefully enough. The moor continued to roll out before them in dreary tones of grey, brown and compost green. Pernikous sat inside the caravan still sulking about his leg. Soon they came to the one source of (semi) fresh water in Yeedlebeetlebeetle, the Yeedlebeetlebeetle River. A small, unnecessary bridge spanned its trickle.

ALL THESE DELAYS ARE REALLY STARTING TO ANNOY ME, ROSY. GET RID OF HIM. I AM NOT COMING OUT UNTIL I'VE FINISHED MY MILO.™

I'M SORRY, BUT I AM AFRAID THE MASTER IS NOT THAT INTIMIDATED BY A MAN WITH PIGTAILS.

PERNIKOUS
DARK MASTER

As they began to cross,
a man walked up to the bridge
from the other side. He stepped forward
as if he wanted to block their path.

Pernikous stuck his head out the
window. 'And who are you?'

'It is I, Olaf Oxthrower, and I am here
to block your path.'

'Another pest,' the necromancer
groaned. 'Run him over, Rosy.'

90

Olaf Oxthrower put a hand to his sword. 'Your sun has set, wizard. Word travels that you fall foul of your own devilment. Your doom shall seal my bargain. Soon Yeedlebeetlebeetle will heel by the boot of its new master, Olaf of the Footheads!'

Footheads were a race of seafaring barbarians who sailed around stirring up trouble. Pernikous squelched out of the caravan and came face to shredded face with the interloper.

'What are you talking about? What bargain?'

YOU'LL NEVER OUT-STARE ME, MEATHEAD. I DON'T EVEN HAVE EYELIDS!

'A curious stranger told me you would cross this bridge. They said that if I slew you, this land would become mine!'

'This curious stranger has me curious,' Pernikous mused. 'But bargain or no bargain, this is *my* county, blondie. Go back to your longboat and shove off.'

Rosy was worried.
Olaf Oxthrower had a
wild look about him.
Goom rubbed his hands
together eagerly. He wondered
what Pernikous would do, and hoped he
wouldn't have enough time to do it.
Seeing his chance, he clambered into the
back of the caravan and began rummaging
through the necromancer's tools.

'Leave the Master alone,' Rosy called to
the Foothead. 'He's on a quest to better
himself!'

Olaf Oxthrower drew his blade. 'I say
thee *nay*, sub-creature! Wizard, prepare to
enter the halls of your
fathers!' And suddenly
he was through talking.
With a swift stroke of his
sword he chopped
Pernikous's head clean
off. It fell to the ground
with a squishy thud.
His body still stood
stupidly in front of it.

AHA! SO THIS IS WHERE
THE MASTER WAS STASHING
ALL HIS NUDIST SOCIETY
MAGAZINES.

Goom reappeared from the caravan with his master's favourite corpse cleaver. 'Now to finish the job!' he yelled, and gave it one heck of a hurl. The cleaver whizzed at the necromancer's headless body.

'Goomy, no!' cried Rosy.

But just as the weapon was about to strike, something most unexpected happened. The body *bent over* to pick up its own head. Instead of skewering the necromancer, the cleaver whizzed *past* Pernikous and got Olaf Oxthrower. THUNK! Right between the eyes. The marauding Foothead fell flat on his back.

Goom hurried over to inspect the damage. Sure enough, Olaf Oxthrower was as dead as a doornail.

Goom kicked himself. 'I got the wrong one...again.'

Rosy shook her head. 'I wish you would cut that out!'

'Nonsense!' came a familiar voice. Pernikous held his skull under his arm. He looked down at the dead Foothead. 'Nice work, Goom. You seem to be the only one in this county *not* trying to kill me.'

Rosy frowned.

Goom laughed nervously. 'All part of the service, Master.'

* GROAN PARTS?

PARTS.

The caravan continued across to the other side of the bridge. Pernikous's head bobbled loosely on top of his shoulders as they went.

...Through the Town...

By evening the caravan trundled into Yeedlebeetlebeetle Town. Shutters slammed and doors bolted as Pernikous passed by. Everyone in town was deathly afraid of what a visit from their local necromancer could mean. By the time the caravan pulled over, you could be forgiven for thinking no one lived in Yeedlebeetlebeetle Town at all.

'Go in and arrange me a room,' Pernikous told Goom. 'And tell the innkeeper I want a table for three ready in the restaurant toot sweet.'

Goom nodded. He went to see the innkeeper while Rosy parked the caravan.

Reading a newspaper at the reception desk was a large white ferret.

'Are you the innkeeper?'

'Yep,' the ferret said from behind his paper.

'Well, can I have a room for the evening?'

He tossed him some keys. 'Here, take any one you want. I don't care.'

'And how about a meal for tonight?'

'It's smorgasbord night, there's plenty there for everyone. Just go into the buffet room.'

'But what if –'

The ferret scowled out from A LITTLE ...CRANKY, ISN'T HE? his paper. 'Look, I don't care about your problems! The inn is here. Use it and leave me alone!'

Goom scratched his head. 'Say, you seem awfully familiar...'

The ferret sighed and went back to his reading. 'It's a long story.'

When evening came the three gathered for dinner. Goom picked a table close to the buffet so they could secure the best grub. He needn't have worried. The only others game enough to dine in the same room as the necromancer were a group of oldies from the retirement castle just outside town.

'I really can't stand those old fogies,' said Pernikous. 'Why can't they cook their own dinner for a change?'

BOOTHS?! THIS IS SUPPOSED TO BE A RESTAURANT. WHERE'S THE CHARM? WHERE'S THE ATMOSPHERE?!

– WHERE'S THE DESSERT TABLE?

MENU

PICKLED DONUTS

'Like you do?' said Goom.

Rosy scolded him. 'Now come on, Goomy. This is going to be a polite dinner. I want us to really try tonight, for the Master's sake. Would you like me to get you anything special, Master?'

'No, that's Goom's job.'

Goom grinned. 'With pleasure, Master.'

The bear recognized a crazy twinkle in Goom's eye. 'Are you sure you don't want *me* to get it for you?'

'Don't trouble yourself, Rosy,' said Goom, hopping over to the buffet table. Rosy watched Goom closely. Just as she had dreaded, he pulled a small vial out of his shoe.

'Why not try some of my "special" dressing, Master?' Goom giggled to himself. He poured a foul black poison all over the roast beast. Then he slopped a thlop of poisoned beast onto a plate. He returned and proudly dished it up.

'There you go, Master. Just what you deserve.'

'Thank you, Goom.'

'No!' Rosy cried. She slapped the plate across the room. 'Don't eat it!'

'Look what you've done!' Pernikous was shocked. 'What's the matter with you?'

Goom scowled at Rosy. She jumped up from the table. 'I'll get you your dinner, Master, please!' Rosy scowled at Goom.

'No,' Pernikous got up. Now it was scowls all round. 'Why don't I get us *both* our dinners?'

He went over to the buffet table and brought back another big slice of roast beast for himself and a blubber pie for Rosy.

'Thank you, Master,' she smiled.

'That pie's not the only thing that smells fishy around here,' he said. 'Bear, you haven't been making any bargains with curious strangers lately, have you?'

'Me, Master? No! Of course not. I'm just as frightened as you about all this.'

'Me, frightened? Are you calling me gutless?'

'I didn't say that, Master, I just meant—'

'Because I'm not gutless, you know. I'm all man!'

'I know Master, I can see your guts from here.'

Pernikous groaned. 'Just shut up and eat your pie.'

Goom began to giggle. 'Your roast beast is getting cold, Master.'

'Fine.'

Goom watched with delight. He'd slyly slipped some more poison onto Pernikous's food while he and Rosy had been busy arguing.

Pernikous sliced a big chunk of beast and shovelled it into his mouth. The meat slid down his slimy throat and into his stomach. As it settled, a strange hissing noise stirred from his innards.

'Sounds like it doesn't agree with you,' said Goom.

The necromancer's middle began to melt. The black acid quickly ate its way through his stomach, his insides fizzling up completely. He looked down at his hollowed-out frame. 'How odd. Maybe I *am* gutless after all.'

IT'S MY VERY OWN RECIPE.

111

Suddenly the White Ferret burst into the room!

'By my giddy Aunt Gertie! What's going on in here?' He pointed to the oldies' table. All of them were face down in their food, their bellies bubbling with acid. Each one was as dead as a doornail.

'I got the wrong one again – again!' Goom hissed.

The ferret went over to the buffet. He took a whiff of the befouled roast beast.

'Pee-yeew! I warned Chef about using leftover leftovers, but he wouldn't listen. This smorgasbord is over!'

The three of them went to bed without finishing their dinner.

...Past the Keep...

Much to the locals' relief, the caravan rumbled out of Yeedlebeetlebeetle Town early next morning. Soon it was back on the road through the moor once more.

Goom was obsessed now. Each failed assassination attempt made him want it even more. Rosy just didn't understand. As soon as the necromancer cured himself they were both finished. Goom was not going to let that happen.

The bear loved her Master. Goom just didn't understand. How could Pernikous possibly get better with the little nut trying to kill him all the time? It was very frustrating.

Pernikous meanwhile had his own worries. Somewhere in Yeedlebeetlebeetle a curious stranger was plotting against him. He was hated by so many people, narrowing it down would take some thought.

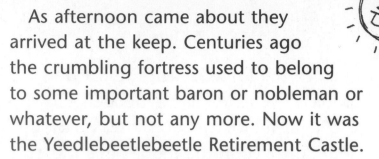

As afternoon came about they arrived at the keep. Centuries ago the crumbling fortress used to belong to some important baron or nobleman or whatever, but not any more. Now it was the Yeedlebeetlebeetle Retirement Castle.

'Retirees,' Pernikous sighed. 'Nothing but useless lingerers.'

Oldies lived in the Yeedlebeetlebeetle Retirement Castle, hidden from the outside world and all its new-fangled ways. The necromancer preferred people to die young. That way their bodies were still fresh and strong. It was much harder making zombies out of withered flesh and brittle bones.

'The Abbey isn't far now. I say we stay here for the night,' said Pernikous.

He went up and hammered on the door.

'Open up, geezers! This is your landlord! I demand lodgings!'

The door unbolted a crack. 'We've paid our taxes,' said a frail voice. 'There's no –'

Pernikous pushed the door open and elbowed the lady aside. 'Get out of the way. Goom, give my bags to this old bag!'

The necromancer settled in for the evening. He picked the best bed in the place, which just happened to be the Castle President's room. By the looks on all the old folks' faces, they were none too happy about it.

'Mrs McMurphy will be back from town soon. When she sees you've taken her room she'll be furious.'

Pernikous laughed at them. 'The old bat's not coming back. She's smorgassed her last 'bord.'

Goom watched as his Master bullied the oldies into fixing his dinner.

'I'm *watching* you, Goomy,' Rosy warned him. She saw a very different Master from the one Goom saw. 'In the old days he would have just fireballed these fogies,' she said, 'but now look. He's talking to them like they're almost human. He's making real progress.'

'Fireballed, hey?' That gave Goom an idea.

Rosy and Goom were given their master's cold leftovers. Then they were told to sleep outside.

'See?' Rosy smiled. 'He's thinking about us.'

Goom just groaned.

Whether the bear liked it or not, the time was right. Goom was going to get *something* hot tonight – a flame-grilled necromancer.

As soon as Rosy was asleep, Goom lit a torch and crept away.

Pernikous's room was high up in the keep. Goom clambered up the outside wall, the torch clamped between his teeth. The night was dark and still and spooky. Finally he reached the right window. He jumped through into his master's bedroom. Pernikous was snoozing away.

'Sweet dreams, Master,' Goom whispered as he held forth the fatal flame.

Suddenly the window slammed open! His torch blew out!

Into the room flapped a large black bat. It had fangs and evil, beady eyes. Goom ducked under the bed in fright.

122

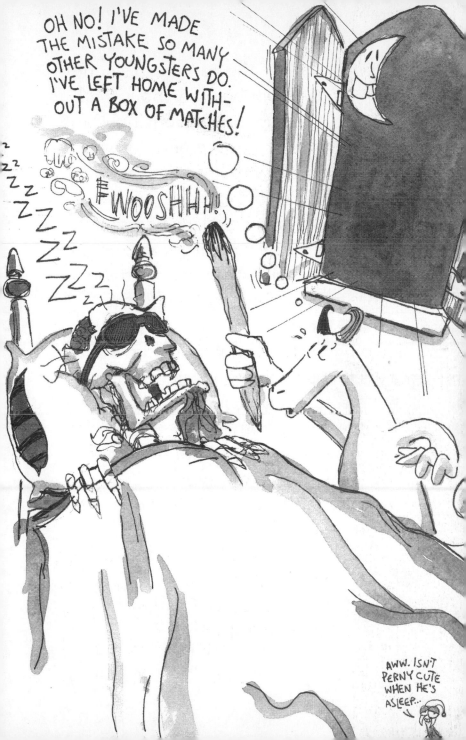

'What is this?' the bat hissed. 'Another in *my* coffin? We shall see about that!'

The bat fell upon Pernikous's neck. Its wicked fangs grew long and hungry.

Suddenly the window burst open again!

Rosy leapt into the darkened room puffing and panting. She saw Goom over Pernikous, obviously trying to strangle him. She grabbed the little psycho around the neck.

'Enough is enough! Leave the Master alone!' Rosy's big paws squeezed until the creature's eyes bugged out. 'I'll throttle you, you maniac!'

Goom jumped out from under the bed. 'Rosy, that's not me!'

ROSY, NO! DON'T TOUCH THAT THING! BATS CARRY DISEASE! (PLUS THEY MAKE YOUR HANDS SMELL ALL 'MOUSY.')

Rosy dropped the bat at the sight of
Goom. The flying rodent flopped on the
floor and returned to its true shape, that
of Yeedlebeetlebeetle Retirement Castle
President, Mrs McMurphy. The old bat
(who now wasn't) lay there gasping
for breath.

'What's going on?' Rosy cried.

'That's what I'd like to know!' Pernikous's bed light blinked on. He was awake. 'Why don't we start with the part where you were going to throttle me!'

'No!' said Rosy. 'I was talking to Goom!'

'You want to kill *him* too?' he glared across at Goom. 'What is *he* doing in here?'

BACK TO THE ABYSS, YOU UNHOLY CREATURE OF THE NIGHT!

'I came to save you, Master,' he said quickly. 'Yes, from this vampire! I saw her fly in your window.' He held up the unlit torch. 'See? Here's my stake!' Goom dashed over and drove it straight through Mrs McMurphy's undead heart.

Pernikous watched her writhe around, scream a few dirty words and then shrivel up to dust. It was standard vampire stuff.

GEE, THE LITTLE FELLA IS PRETTY HANDY WITH THAT STAKE. HE TAKES AFTER MY OWN UNDEAD TAMING ABILITIES, I GUESS.

iD SAY MORE LIKE TOO MUCH LATE NIGHT TEE-VEE.

'And *you* tried to stop him,' he scowled at Rosy. 'You *are* in league with the curious stranger, aren't you?'

Goom suddenly noticed something outside the window. 'This discussion can wait,' he pointed.

Pernikous got up and looked.

'Of course! No wonder these fogies never seem to die.'

The keep's courtyard was swarming with undead bloodsuckers. All the retirees had transformed into unholy creatures of the night.

'Killing their leader may not have been a good idea,' Goom shuddered. 'Looks like the three of us are dead as doornails now!'

'Oh, I wouldn't say that,' said Pernikous. He knew exactly what to do. After all, he *was* a necromancer. The slimy fellow reached under his pillow and brought out his sawn-off shotgun.

'Where did you get *that* from?' Rosy asked. Her mind boggled.

Goom was flabbergasted. 'Is that thing legal in this county?'

'It is if you own the place,' Pernikous said as he cocked the shotgun. 'With that curious stranger around, I thought I'd best keep it handy.' He kicked open the bedroom door. 'Now, let's rock and roll!'

Things got a little wild at Yeedlebeetlebeetle Retirement Castle that night. Maybe *too* wild for some of its older residents. Pernikous, though – he had a blastin' good time.

DON'T TRY THIS AT HOME, KIDS.

...And to the Cliffs...

Garlic-coated buckshot did the trick nicely. Pernikous ran about, gun blazing. Soon vampire guts coated the walls and vampire brains rolled down the halls. And when the biggest, oldest, ugliest vampire, Mr McMurphy, confronted him in the castle rumpus room, Pernikous wasn't ready to slow down.

'Your wicked wife has already been Swiss-cheesed,' he said. 'What makes you think you'll fare differently?'

'Because before you got here we made a deal with someone. If we finish you this county is ours!'

Pernikous spat. 'I'm so sick of this curious stranger stirring things up! What gives him the right to say who gets title over Yeedlebeetlebeetle anyway?'

'Who said anything about them being a *he*?' said Mr McMurphy as he leapt at Pernikous, fangs gleaming.

Naturally Pernikous let him have it. He blasted a hole in the bloodsucker so big, he could have used him as a hula hoop.

'It's exactly what these fogies deserved,' he remarked. 'The nerve – they only drank blood but *still* they'd come into town to raid the smorgasbord. Nothing but sheer greed!'

By sunrise the fun was over. The vintage vamps were no match for the necromancer's twelve-gauge pump-action. The entire community got blasted undeader than a doornail. Pernikous really enjoyed it. A shotgun rampage was the ideal therapy. Now he felt much more like his old, insanely evil self.

He'd become separated from Goom and Rosy when he ran amok. As he gathered up a few spare parts, he couldn't find his servants anywhere.

He decided there was only one possible reason why.

'Of course, it all adds up! That bear – the curious stranger has got to her too! She's taken Goom and is trying to beat me to the Abbey of the Broken Heart!'

Pernikous dashed off across the moor as fast as his slimy form could carry him.

He was right too. Well, sort of. His servants *had* raced off to the abbey, but not because of any stranger. Goom was bent on finding the cure first and destroying it. And Rosy, as slow as she was, had to stop Goom before he could stop Pernikous.

The Abbey of the Broken Heart stood high on the Yeedlebeetlebeetle Cliffs. The old stone church had been there for countless windswept years and seemed all but deserted.

Goom was first to arrive. He raced along the clifftop road to the abbey. Waves smashed against the rocks beneath him. He charged at the doors, but they were locked tight. A little sign read: WEEKLY MASS 9 AM SUNDAY – SPREAD PEACE.

'Sunday?' Goom gasped. 'I can't wait that long!'

'Stand aside,' came a voice behind him.

Goom turned around. The necromancer stood there, holding his shotgun.

'No, Master! It's locked.'

Pernikous laughed. 'I'll do just as it commands then, by spreading it to pieces!' And with a blunderbussing boom he blasted the door to bits.

'Now it's time to find this "rare and mysterious magic". I'll be cured before the day is out.'

Goom couldn't stand it any longer. A rage suddenly boiled up inside him, a stew of torment and tyranny, a foul ferment of fear and frustration. This was his last chance. He leapt at his Master, his fingers spidering around his throat.

'You *won't* be cured!' Goom cried. 'I won't let you! This is the end for you, you wart-ridden, weasel-faced, garlic-breathed, badly-dressed, greasy-haired, bow-legged, pot-bellied, **pigeon-toed PINHEAD!**'

Suddenly it all came back to Pernikous. Goom's words jolted his memory like a lightning bolt.

'It was YOU!' he gagged. '*You* did this to me! *You* pushed me down the well!'

'And I'll do it again!' Goom hollered. 'You beat me and bully me and treat me like garbage! I've had it! You're going down!'

Pernikous staggered back. Beneath them the sea churned like a hungry monster waiting to be fed. The necromancer wrenched his familiar off him and held him over his head.

'You've had it all right, Goom! But *you're* the one's who's going down – over the cliff!'

'Master, no!' Goom squirmed desperately, but Pernikous's bony grip was too tight.

But just as he was about to fall, Goom felt himself lifted even higher.

Rosy had arrived just in time!

The big bear grabbed Pernikous and lifted him over her head.

'*That's enough!*' she roared.

'Rosy, no!' they both cried.

'I should throw *the two* of you over! You're both so full of hate and spite and bile! I was a fool to think either of you would ever change. Goom, you've been a menace ever since you were born, and you, Master, I should let him loose on you because you deserve it! You're a vicious, cruel, old devil! I think I'll do Yeedlebeetlebeetle the biggest favour of all and get rid of you both!'

But the Abbey told her to stop.

'STOP!'

Rosy turned, still holding Pernikous, who was still holding Goom. They were absolutely dumbfounded.

'Did it... ' gasped Rosy.

'Just... ' gasped Pernikous.

'Speak?' gasped Goom.

The old Abbey groaned to life like a waking giant. Its head was the belfry and its body was the chapel. Stone grated against stone as it turned to look down at the feud before it.

'I AM THE ABBEY OF THE BROKEN HEART.'

...Where Stands the Abbey of the Broken Heart

'Now *that's* rare and mysterious,' staggered Pernikous. They let go of one another. They all felt a bit stupid for the display they'd just put on.

'A talking building?' Goom couldn't believe it.

'WHAT DID YOU EXPECT?' The

Abbey spoke low and slow,
like a voice rising up from a well.

'Well, maybe a divine scroll or a
saintly spirit, you know, church-type stuff.'

'ARE YOU SAYING I'M NOT
CHURCHY ENOUGH?'

Pernikous butted in. 'Look, we'll deal
with *your* insecurities later. Right now I'm
the one with the problem.'

'YES. I KNOW WHY YOU ARE HERE.
YOUR BROKEN HEART.'

'My broken *whole body*, you mean. Look at me. I'm a freak! I'm here for you to cure me.'

YOU ARE NOT THE FIRST TO COME TO ME WITH SUCH A REQUEST. I HAVE BEEN PROMISED A DEAL . . . '

Pernikous crossed him arms. 'If you say you've made some bargain with a curious stranger, I am going to scream.'

'I am no stranger,' said a sudden voice. A shambling shape shuffled out from behind the abbey's legs. 'I am your *wife*!'

Everyone gasped (even the Abbey, who already knew she was there).

'EX-wife, EX-wife!' Pernikous barked. 'I should've known!'

Goom was shocked. 'Geraldine the sewing machine! The Master's luscious lost zombie lover! I thought you'd run away.'

'Not exactly,' Geraldine ambled forward. She was a woman in pieces. Half her head was missing, her sexy sewing machine body was all broken and she had old bedsprings for arms.

'You and Rosy never knew that your Master and I were secretly married. He pledged his eternal love to me one night after a red-hot make-out session up at Inspiration Moor.'

'Ewww!' Goom poked out his tongue. 'That's gross!'

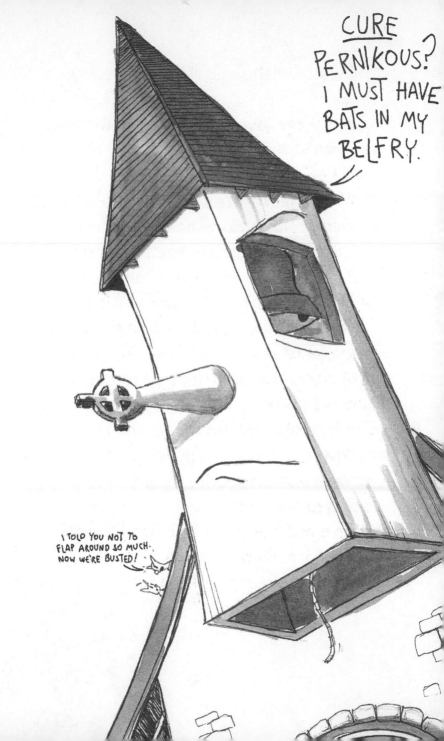

Geraldine showed Rosy her wedding ring.

'Oh, how lovely,' the bear said. 'Are those real diamonds?'

'Of course they are!' said Pernikous. 'I'm no cheapskate. Anyhow, I told you Geraldine: that ring means nothing!'

'Yes, it does. Under Yeedlebeetlebeetle County Law it's proof that our vows of love are binding. You *are* my husband, which means that I'm just as much landlord of these moors as you are. And if you die, they all go to me!'

'So that's why you set all those cretins after me! On a promise to give them the deed to Yeedlebeetlebeetle. How could you?'

...OH YEH...

Geraldine fumed. 'It's nothing compared to the way you dismantled me in my sleep on our honeymoon night!'

'Oh no,' Rosy shook her head. 'Master, how low can you get?'

'But I had to,' he explained. 'It was only on that night I realised she suddenly owned half of everything. I had to get rid of her, so I took her apart and chucked her down the well. Yeedlebeetlebeetle is mine, mine, MINE!'

Geraldine went on. 'The well brought me back to life, but I was still a mess, just like your precious master is now. My memory was a haze. My heart was broken, but I didn't know why. I staggered blindly around the county, distraught and alone. Finally I found myself here, the only place that seemed to fit my predicament – The Abbey of the Broken Heart. And last Sunday at mass, when Eva Braunstein told me what she'd seen in her crystal ball about your own little mishap, that jogged my mind just enough. I turned to the church for salvation. '

Pernikous sneered. 'And I suppose that's where you step in?'

The Abbey nodded.

'YES. I HEALED HER MEMORY. IN RETURN SHE MADE ME, AND ANYONE ELSE WHO WAS INTERESTED, A BARGAIN. KILL THE NECROMANCER AND BECOME LANDLORD OF ALL VEEDLEBEETLEBEETLE.'

'Kill me?' Pernikous said. 'But aren't you supposed to cure me?'

'THERE IS ONLY ONE CURE FOR YOU, PERNIKOUS!'

And the
Abbey
stepped
on him.

AND THEY ALL LIVED HAPPILY EVER AFTER...SORT OF

The Abbey of the Broken Heart did get hold of the county deed, but as Goom had already found out, zombie Pernikous was tough to finish off completely. The Abbey didn't quite kill him, but it took the necromancer several months of intense physical and mental therapy to recover from being squashed. He spent most of it bedridden back at his tower.

DOES THIS LOOK LIKE HAPPY ENDING TO YOU?!

RGH! I THOUGHT I SAID NO CHARACTERS FROM OTHER BOOKS?

CAN'T YOU READ, OLAF? GOOM HAS CHANGED HIS HOMICIDAL WAYS NOW!

WELL, I... ..UMM..

PRIMARY SCHOOL STICKLER, MEGAN FITZGERALD.

GOOM

Fortunately though, he did have someone to care for him. Rosy helped him do his exercises and cooked him his apple mush and strained carrots. Goom helped by not trying to assassinate him any more.

Geraldine moved back in too. Seeing Pernikous crushed and disgusting made her realise that at last they could relate to each other. Like a good wife, she decided to overlook the fact that her man was a loser and love him anyway.

She used the parts Pernikous had collected on his journey to repair herself. Soon she was returned to her original zombie sex goddess shape, if such a thing were possible. She ran the household and made sure everyone was happy. You could almost say Pernikous *was* cured. He was still a shredded skeleton of a man, but like a good husband, he knew he had to obey his woman or he'd never hear the end of it.

Pernikous went on being a
necromancer, but the days of undead
tax collectors and ghouls roaming the
countryside were over.

Yeedlebeetlebeetle had nothing to
fear from him anymore. The county's
new owner kept everyone on the
straight and narrow. He even allowed
a church wedding ceremony for
Pernikous and Geraldine.

To be realistic though,
a supernaturally animated
abbey could never run a
county all by itself.
So what was the solution?
Goom, of course.
He became the Archbishop
of Yeedlebeetlebeetle.

AMEN.